A Garden

Illustrated by Philip Webb

Rigby

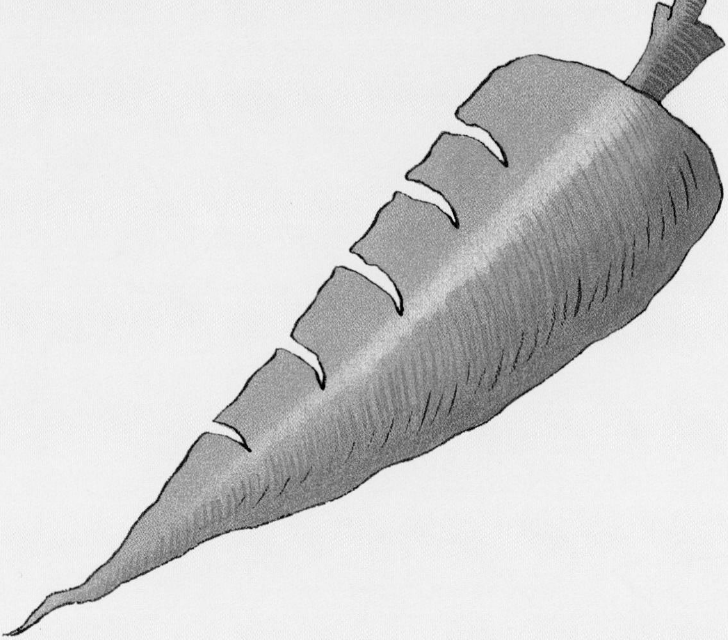

a carrot

a bean

a pumpkin

a tomato

a strawberry

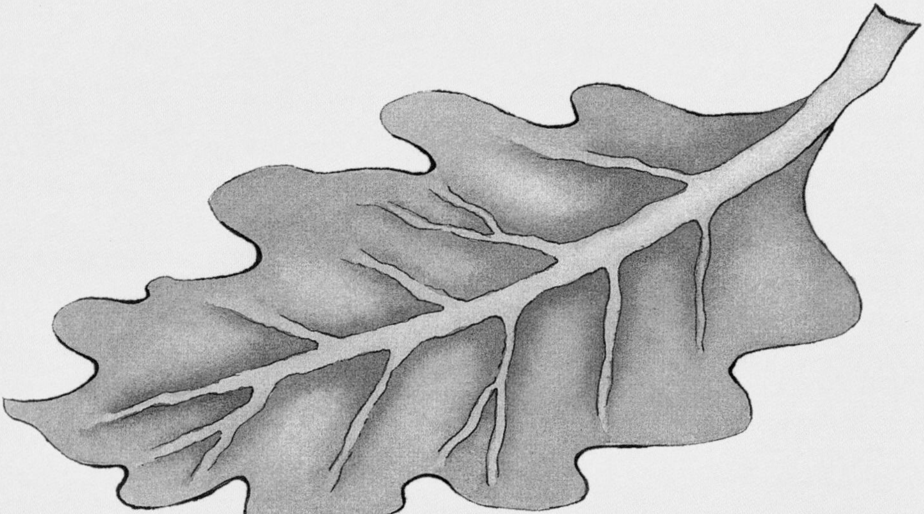

a leaf

a carrot
a bean
a strawberry

a pumpkin
a leaf
a tomato

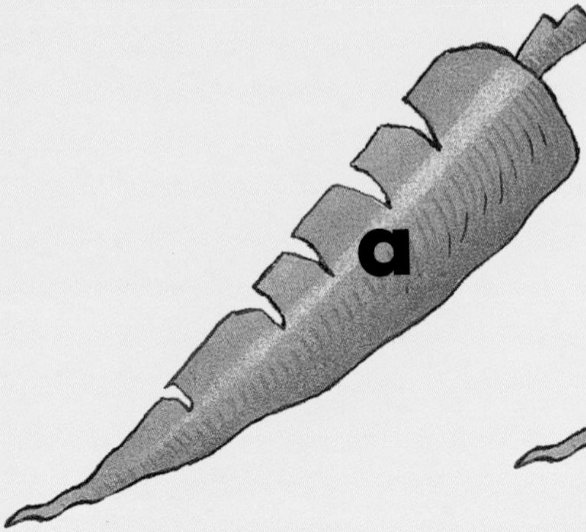
a

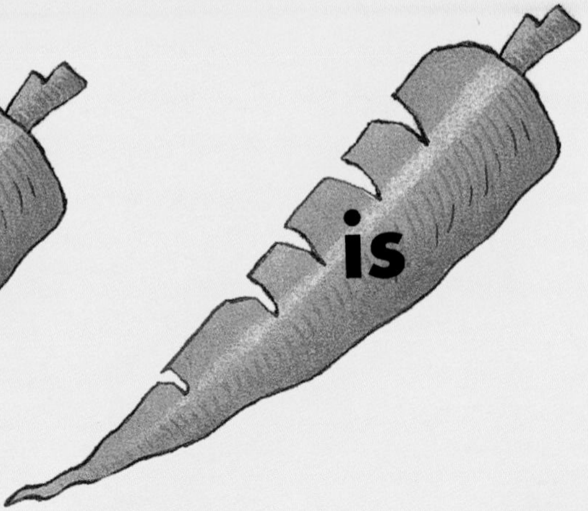
is

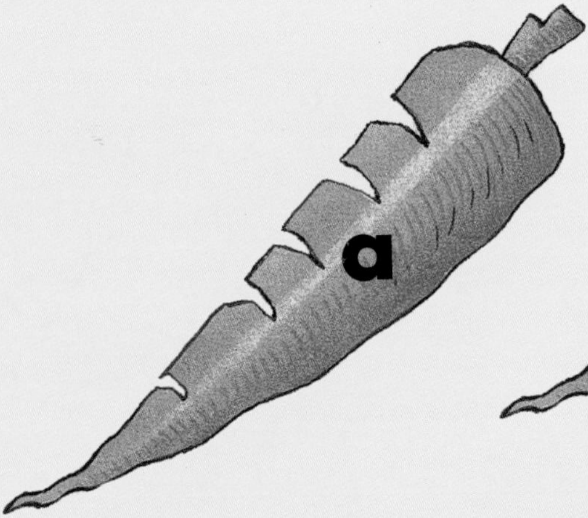
a

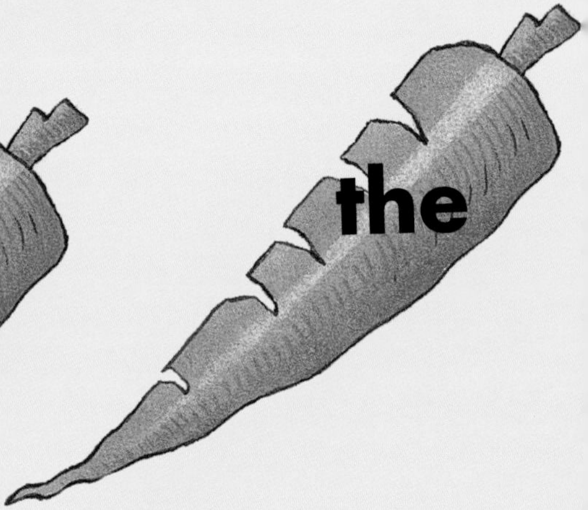
the

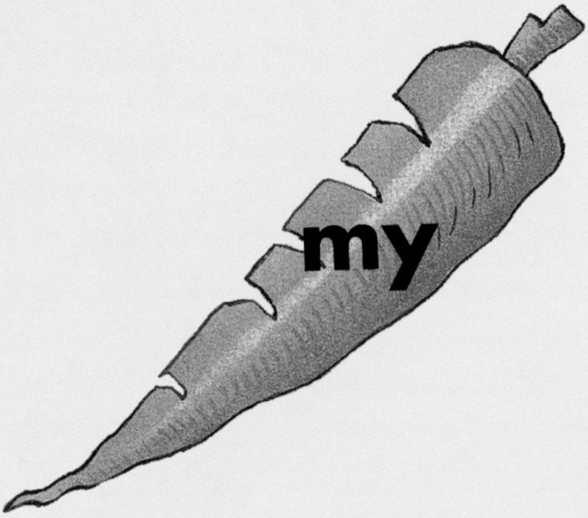
my